Ava
the Sunset
Fairy

Special thanks to Narinder Dhami

No part of this work may be reproduced, stored in a retrieval system, or transmitted in any form or by any means, electronic, mechanical, photocopying, recording, or otherwise, without written permission of the publisher. For information regarding permission, write to Rainbow Magic Limited c/o HIT Entertainment, 830 South Greenville Avenue, Allen, TX 75002-3320.

ISBN 978-0-545-27044-1

12 11 10 9 8 7 6 5 4 3 2 1   11 12 13 14 15/0

Printed in the U.S.A.   40

This edition first printing, July 2011

Ava
the Sunset
Fairy

by Daisy Meadows

SCHOLASTIC INC.

New York   Toronto   London   Auckland
Sydney   Mexico City   New Delhi   Hong Kong

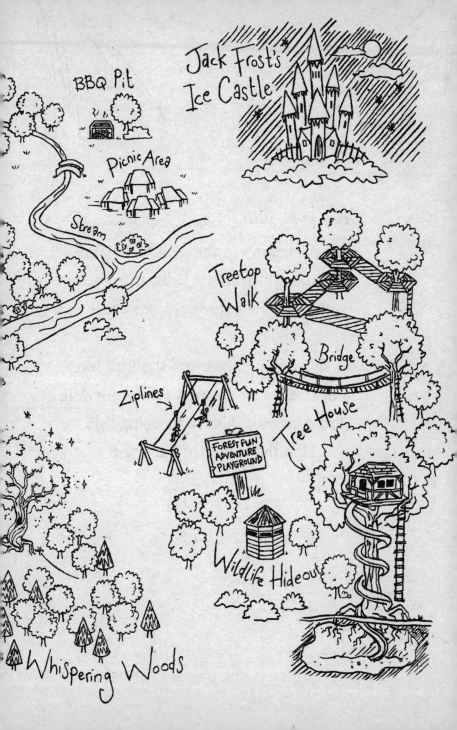

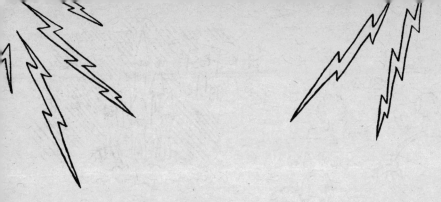

The Night Fairies' special magic powers
Bring harmony to the nighttime hours.
But now their magic belongs to me,
And I'll cause chaos, you shall see!

In sunset, moonlight, and starlight, too,
There'll be no more sweet dreams for you.
From evening dusk to morning light,
I am the master of the night!

Contents

Strange Sunset   1

Twilight Tent   11

Jack Frost's Plan   23

Two Greedy Boys   37

In the Whispering Woods   47

Green Dust   59

Strange Sunset

"Look, Kirsty!" Rachel Walker said excitedly to her best friend, Kirsty Tate. It was a warm summer evening, and the girls were standing on the deck of a little red-and-white ferry as it chugged along the winding river. "I don't think we're far from Camp Stargaze now."

Kirsty looked where Rachel was pointing and saw a wooden sign on the river bank. The sign was in the shape of an arrow pointing downriver and it said: THIS WAY TO CAMP STARGAZE.

"Hooray!" Kirsty beamed at Rachel. "I'm *really* looking forward to this vacation."

The girls and their parents were spending a week of summer break at Camp Stargaze together. Kirsty and Rachel were thrilled. Even though they were best friends, they didn't live near each other. They loved meeting up during school breaks whenever they could!

"It's not far now, girls," called Mr. Walker, Rachel's dad. He was standing at the bow of the boat with Mrs. Walker

and Mr. and Mrs. Tate, watching the beautiful countryside pass by. The river was surrounded by open fields and rolling hills, with green trees here and there.

"Oh, look, girls!" Mrs. Tate exclaimed, gazing up at the sky. "The sun is setting. Isn't it pretty?"

All the passengers on deck, including
Rachel and Kirsty, looked up, too. The
sun was just beginning to sink slowly,
streaking the blue sky with long ribbons
of gold, orange, and pink. The light
reflected down, bathing the fields and
trees in a soft glow. The water looked
like liquid gold!

"It's magical!" Rachel said with a sigh. Then she glanced at Kirsty and flashed a secret smile her way.

Kirsty grinned back, knowing exactly what Rachel was thinking. She and Rachel knew  more about magic than anyone else in the whole world. They were friends with the fairies!

The girls had visited Fairyland many times, and had helped their magical friends whenever they were in trouble. The fairies' biggest enemy was mean, grumpy Jack Frost. He was always trying to cause trouble—in Fairyland *and* the human world. Rachel and Kirsty were never sure what problems Jack Frost and his goblins would cause next!

Suddenly Kirsty blinked. For a moment, she thought the gold, orange, and pink colors of the setting sun were fading and changing into something else.

I must be imagining it, Kirsty thought. But then she looked again and was horrified to see that she was right! The beautiful colors *were* changing before Kirsty's eyes!

"What's happening?" Rachel asked. She'd noticed exactly the same thing, and so had everyone else on the ferry.

They were all staring up at the sky
in surprise.

"Look at the sunset," Kirsty
cried. "It's turning *green*!"
A few seconds later,
all the gold, pink,
and orange had
vanished completely.
Now the sunset was
casting a strange,
spooky green glow
on the landscape
around it.
"Everything's green!"
Kirsty added in a
shocked voice. "The sun,
the fields, the ferry—everything!"
"And so are *we*!" Rachel pointed out,
staring at Kirsty. All of the passengers,

including the girls and their parents,
were bathed in the same emerald glow.

"We look like Jack Frost's goblins!"
Kirsty whispered.

The girls' parents and the
other grown-ups on
the ferry were
discussing
what could
have caused
the strange
sunset.

"Maybe it's
just a trick of the
light shining through the clouds," Mr.
Tate suggested.

"Or the sunset could be reflecting off
the river and the fields, picking up that
green color," said Mrs. Walker.

Looking puzzled, Rachel glanced at Kirsty. "I think there's something very strange going on here, Kirsty," she murmured.

"So do I," Kirsty agreed. "I wonder if it could be something *magical*?"

Twilight Tent

"Here we are," called the captain of the ferry as it docked at a small wooden pier. "Welcome to Camp Stargaze."

As they waited to climb off the ferry, Rachel and Kirsty looked toward the shore and saw the prettiest campsite.

There was a sign with WELCOME TO CAMP STARGAZE painted on it in silver letters. Beyond that, the girls could see large tents pitched on the grass at the edge of a green forest. The tents all had different names painted on wooden signs outside the entrances. They were surrounded by colorful flowerbeds, and a sparkling stream flowed through the campsite on its way to the river. There were plenty of open spaces for games and activities, and lots of picnic tables scattered all around. The girls were also excited to see a small white

building with a dome on top of it.

"Remember I told you the camp directors chose this location because you can get really clear views of the night sky and constellations from here?" Mrs. Tate said to Rachel and Kirsty. "That white building is the observatory. There's a telescope inside of it for looking at the stars."

"I can't wait!" Rachel said with a grin, and Kirsty nodded in agreement.

"Camp Stargaze is beautiful, isn't it, girls?" Mr. Walker remarked as they picked up their luggage. "It's too bad this sunset is making everything look green."

The camp counselors were waiting on the dock. They had their clipboards to check everyone in. As the Walkers and the Tates climbed off the ferry, one of the counselors stepped forward.

"Hi, I'm Peter," he said with a smile. "Welcome to Camp Stargaze. Now, let's find out which tent you'll be staying in."

Peter checked his clipboard and told the Walkers and Tates that they were in the Twilight Tent. Then he gave them a map of the campsite and pointed them in the right direction.

"The Twilight Tent," Rachel repeated
as they walked past the welcome sign
and into the camp. "That sounds so
pretty." Rachel loved twilight, that hazy
time of day just before night falls.

There were lots of other families
settling in and some, like the Walkers
and Tates, were walking around
searching for their tents.

"Is it this one?" Kirsty stopped to read a sign outside a cream-colored tent. "Nope, this is the Moonlight Tent."

"There it is!" Rachel said excitedly as she spotted a sign that said THE TWILIGHT TENT.

The girls were thrilled to see that their tent was the color of the night sky, a deep midnight blue, with tiny silver stars scattered all over it. The tent was enormous! There were three separate sleeping areas—one bedroom for each set of parents and one for Rachel and Kirsty to share. There was also a small kitchen and a living area at the front of the tent.

"This is great!" Kirsty grinned at Rachel as they tried out the cots in their bedroom. "The tent's almost as big as a house."

Mrs. Walker ducked her head in at that moment. "There's a bathroom with toilets and showers just a short walk away," she told them. "Why don't you two explore the rest of the camp while we unpack? We'll see you for the cookout later."

THE TWILIGHT TENT

"OK, Mom," Rachel said. "Let's go, Kirsty."

The girls left their bags in the bedroom and wandered into the campsite. Just outside their tent, a group of kids of all ages was gathered around Peter, the camp counselor the girls had met earlier. They were staring up at the sky. It was still a deep green! Rachel and Kirsty went to join them.

"Isn't it strange that the sun hasn't set yet?" Peter said with a frown. "It should be dark by now."

The girls had been so excited about arriving at Camp Stargaze, they hadn't really noticed that the sun had stopped setting. But now they could see that the sun didn't seem to have dropped any lower in the green sky.

"Have you had a green sunset here before, Peter?" asked one of the boys in the group.

Peter shook his head. "Never!" he replied. "I have no idea what's causing it."

Kirsty glanced at Rachel. "There really *is* something weird going on," she remarked.

Rachel didn't reply because something had caught her eye. It was a tiny patch of golden light in the middle of the green sunset. As she stared at it, the

light seemed to grow brighter and more
sparkly.

"Kirsty!" Rachel nudged her friend.
"Can you see that little ray of light, right
in the middle of all the green?"

Kirsty looked and nodded. "Is it a
star?" she asked.

As Rachel and Kirsty watched in
wonder, they saw the burst of sparkling
light swirl down from the sky and swoop
toward the river. None of the other
campers noticed.

"Quick, let's find out what it is!"
Rachel whispered to Kirsty.

Just as the girls reached the bank of
the river, the dazzling light skimmed
across the water toward them. It landed
in a shimmer of sparkles on top of the
WELCOME TO CAMP STARGAZE sign.

"Kirsty!" Rachel cried, her eyes
shining with excitement. "It's a fairy!"

Jack Frost's Plan

The tiny fairy was out of breath after her speedy flight. She looked around to make sure none of the other campers could see her, and then she waved at Rachel and Kirsty.

"Hi, girls," she said between breaths. "We haven't met before, but I've seen you lots of times in Fairyland! I'm Ava the Sunset Fairy, one of the Night Fairies."

Thrilled, Rachel and Kirsty rushed
over to Ava, who fluttered down to perch
on Kirsty's shoulder. Ava wore a beaded
dress in soft shades of sunset
pink and orange, and
sparkly ballet flats with
ankle straps. Her long,
wavy auburn hair was
pulled back from her
face with a glittery
pink clip.

"Why are you here,
Ava?" Kirsty asked.

"Is it because of the weird, green
sunset?" Rachel wanted to know.

Ava's face fell. "Yes," she said sadly.
"I can't *believe* what Jack Frost has done
this time!"

Rachel and Kirsty glanced at each

other with concern.

"Jack Frost's up to his old tricks again?" Rachel groaned.

"Girls, will you help me and the other Night Fairies fix everything?" Ava asked them anxiously. "It's such a mess. We can't do it without you."

Immediately, Rachel and Kirsty nodded.

"What happened, Ava?" asked Kirsty.

Ava sighed. "It's a long story, so the quickest way to explain it is for you to come back to Fairyland with me," she replied. "You can meet the other six Night Fairies, and we can show you exactly what happened. Will you come, girls?"

"Of course we will!" Rachel and Kirsty exclaimed. The girls knew that, as always, time would stand still while they were in Fairyland, so their parents wouldn't realize they were gone.

Looking very relieved, Ava lifted her wand and surrounded the two girls with a cloud of magic fairy dust. Rachel and Kirsty closed their eyes as they were whisked off their feet. They felt themselves rushing quickly through the air.

"Here we are," Ava called. "Welcome back to Fairyland."

Rachel and Kirsty opened their eyes. They were standing in the beautiful garden of the Fairyland Palace. Waiting to greet them were King Oberon, Queen Titania, and six other fairies.

"Girls, once again you've answered our call for help," Queen Titania said gratefully, moving forward to hug Rachel, then Kirsty. "We're so glad to see you."

"And so are the Night Fairies," King Oberon added, nodding at the six fairies standing beside him. "You've already met Ava, and here are Lexi the Firefly Fairy, Zara the Starlight Fairy, Morgan the Midnight Fairy, Nia the Night Owl Fairy, Anna the Moonbeam Fairy, and Sabrina the Sweet Dreams Fairy."

"Our Night Fairies make sure everything that happens between dusk and dawn goes smoothly, in both the fairy and human worlds," explained Queen Titania. "But now Jack Frost and his goblins have ruined the nighttime!"

"How?" Kirsty asked.

"We'll show you exactly what happened in the Seeing Pool," Ava said.

The king and queen led the way through the garden to the magical pool. The surface of the water was smooth and glasslike, but when Queen Titania waved her wand over it, the pool began to swirl gently. A few seconds later, pictures appeared in the water. Rachel and Kirsty stared closely and saw a beautiful pink-and-gold bedroom with seven little beds.

"You can see the Night Fairies' bedroom in their cottage," the queen told them. When the door opened, Ava and the other six fairies fluttered into their bedroom. The girls noticed that each fairy was holding a small, satin drawstring bag, each one in a different color. "There are seven different colors of bags," said Ava, "and seven different kinds of fairy dust—one for every Night Fairy. You can see that we keep them under our pillows."

In the Seeing Pool, the fairies were now putting their magic bags underneath their silk pillowcases. Then, looking excited, they hurried out of the bedroom again.

"We were on our way to a party under the stars last night with all our fairy friends," Ava explained. "But look what happened while we were gone. . . ."

Rachel and Kirsty gazed at the Seeing Pool again. Suddenly, Jack Frost and a crowd of goblins blew in through the open window, riding on a blast of icy wind.

"I want those bags!" Jack Frost yelled.
"Hurry up and steal them before those
silly Night Fairies come back!"

The scattered in all directions. They
threw the pillows off the beds and
grabbed the satin bags. Then they
held them up triumphantly to show
Jack Frost.

Next, one of the
goblins picked
up a pillow with
his free hand.
Laughing to
himself, he
smacked the
closest goblin
over the head
with it. The
second goblin

roared with anger and grabbed another pillow to hit him back.

Soon all the goblins were having a pillow fight! They whacked each other so hard that the pillows burst, and tiny, fluffy white feathers flew everywhere, making a huge mess. Rachel and Kirsty looked at each other in dismay.

"Enough!" Jack Frost roared furiously. The goblins dropped their pillows, looking very guilty. They stood still and clutched the bags, waiting for an order from Jack Frost.

"With the Night Fairies' magic, I can cause nighttime chaos *everywhere*," Jack Frost bragged. "But we have to hide the bags in the human world."

He pointed his wand at the goblins. An ice bolt sped toward them and swept

the goblins off their feet. Then it zoomed
out the window, taking the goblins and
the Night Fairies' magic bags with it.

Jack Frost looked extremely proud of
himself.

"Usually I hate the nighttime," he
muttered. "But now I can control
everything that happens between dusk
and dawn, and things are going to be
different!" With a cackle of laughter, he

headed back to his Ice Castle.

"Without our special magic, nothing will go right. It will be nonstop trouble from dusk until dawn!" Ava told Rachel and Kirsty. "Will you two help me find my bag of sunbeam dust?"

Rachel and Kirsty nodded eagerly.

"But why does Jack Frost want to disrupt the nighttime so much?" asked Kirsty, looking puzzled.

"We don't know," Queen Titania replied, "but we have to stop him!" She lifted her sparkling wand. "Girls, I need to send you and Ava back to Camp Stargaze right now. The bags will have become bigger in the human world, so they'll be easier to find. Good luck."

"Good luck!" echoed the other fairies as the queen showered Ava, Kirsty, and

Rachel with magic fairy dust.

Rachel and Kirsty waved, feeling very excited. Another wonderful fairy adventure was about to begin!

Two Greedy Boys

Just a few seconds later, Rachel and
Kirsty were back at Camp Stargaze,
standing by the welcome sign. Ava was
hovering next to them. Everything was
still covered in the same green glow, and
the sun remained high in the sky.

Ava frowned. "The sun won't set again until I find my bag of sunbeam dust," she sighed. "I can sense that it's around here somewhere."

"We'll do our best to find it, Ava," Kirsty promised.

"The cookout's starting," Rachel said. The camp counselors had set up tables and were putting big bowls of salad and plates of sandwich buns on them. Peter,

 wearing a chef's hat, was watching over a large grill and flipping the burgers every once in a while.

"We'd better go and find our parents," said Kirsty. "They'll

be wondering where we are."

Ava nodded and fluttered into Rachel's pocket so she'd be out of sight. The girls hurried across the campsite toward their parents, who were just joining the end of the food line.

"Ah, there you are, girls." Mr. Tate handed Rachel and Kirsty each a plate. "We were wondering where you'd gone."

"This looks great, doesn't it?" Mrs. Walker said, admiring the big bowls of salad and wide variety of sandwiches.

Rachel and Kirsty nodded.

"I hope this doesn't take too long, though," Rachel whispered to Kirsty as they waited in line. "I want to start looking for Ava's bag of sunbeam dust!"

But to the girls' dismay, the line *was* moving very slowly. Rachel and Kirsty soon realized that it was because of two boys who were just ahead of them.

The boys were wearing sunhats, big T-shirts, and baggy cargo shorts. They helped themselves to lots of food from all the different bowls, and carried as much as they could.

"They must be hungry!" Kirsty murmured. She and Rachel watched as the boys wobbled over to the picnic tables

on the far side of the campsite, clutching
their armfuls of food.

Then Rachel nudged Kirsty.

"Look at their noses and their feet!"
she whispered in her friend's ear.

Kirsty stared at the two boys as they
sat down at the picnic table farthest
away from everyone else and began to
chow down. They looked green, but so

did everyone else at the camp because of the glow of the sunset. However, these two boys also had long pointed noses and very big feet.

"Goblins!" Kirsty murmured.

"I wonder if they have Ava's bag of sunbeam dust?" said Rachel. "We have to find out, Kirsty!"

Rachel and Kirsty quickly picked out their own dinner and then asked their parents if they could sit with some of the other kids.

Their parents agreed, so the girls hurried over to the

picnic table next to the goblins. Some of the kids they'd met earlier were there, and they were talking about the activities at camp. Rachel and Kirsty joined in, but at the same time they were listening to what the goblins at the next table were saying.

"Give that burger back!" one of the goblins yelled. "It's mine!"

"No way!" answered the other goblin, taking a big bite out of it.

The first goblin made a face at him. "Do

you still have that bag of fairy dust in your pocket?" he demanded.

The girls glanced at each other.

"Of course I do," the second goblin said grumpily through a mouthful of food. "I'm way too smart to lose something as important as *that*!" He shoved his hand into the pocket of his cargo shorts, but then he frowned. "The bag's gone!" he groaned. "I must have dropped it."

"Let me see!" the other goblin demanded. He scrambled across the bench and grabbed his friend, turning his pockets inside out. The other goblin growled in protest.

"You did lose it, you fool!" the first goblin cried, poking the other in the ribs with a breadstick. "What's Jack Frost going to say when he finds out? We're in big trouble."

Kirsty turned to Rachel. "We need to find Ava's bag of sunbeam dust before the goblins do!" she whispered.

In the Whispering Woods

"Let's eat our food and then we can start searching the campsite," Rachel suggested. The goblins continued to greedily gobble their dinner, still grumbling about the missing sunbeam dust. Rachel and Kirsty finished eating, but before they had a chance to start their search, Peter called all the kids together.

"Since the sun hasn't set yet, we can stay up a little later and play a game," he announced. The kids cheered. "How about hide-and-seek in the Whispering Woods?" He pointed to the forest at the edge of the campsite.

"Perfect!" Rachel murmured to Kirsty. "We'll be able to hunt for Ava's bag while we play, and no one will guess what we're up to!"

"Now go and hide." Peter covered his eyes and started counting.

"One, two, three . . ."

Rachel, Kirsty, and the others ran
toward the Whispering Woods. Kirsty
glanced back and saw that the two
goblins were still at the picnic table,
stuffing themselves with food.

"At least the goblins won't be looking
for the bag yet," she told Rachel.
"They're too busy eating!"

Once the girls were
in the woods, Ava
peeked out of
Rachel's pocket.
She checked that
there was no one
around, and then
flew out.

"Great job
spotting those

goblins, girls!" Ava cried. "I *know* my bag of sunbeam dust is very close by. We have to find it."

Quickly Ava, Rachel, and Kirsty began to search around the trees. Suddenly they heard Peter shout, "Ready or not, here I come!"

Kirsty looked worried. "We'd better hide," she said. "If Peter finds us, we'll be out of the game and we'll have to go back to camp before we've really searched the woods well."

Kirsty and Rachel hurried toward a large, thick bush. As they reached it, Ava suddenly gave a squeal of surprise.

"There's already someone hiding there!" she whispered, diving out of sight behind Kirsty's hair.

Rachel and Kirsty saw Alex, one of

the other campers, waving at them from behind the bush. "Come on," she said with a smile, motioning to them. "There's plenty of room!"

The girls slipped behind the bush to join her. Almost immediately, they heard footsteps.

"Shh!" Alex put her finger to her lips. "That might be Peter."

But it wasn't. Rachel and Kirsty glanced at each other with disappointment as they peeked through the leaves and saw the outline of a pointy nose. It was a goblin— the one who'd lost the bag!

"Hurry up and hide," Alex called to

the goblin. "Peter's coming!"

"I'm not playing that silly game," the goblin replied grumpily. "I'm looking for something very important!" And he moved on.

"I hear more footsteps," Alex warned Rachel and Kirsty.

A moment later Peter walked by, but he didn't notice them. Alex gave a sigh of relief.

"I'm going to go find my friend Katie and hide with her," she told the girls. "Do you want to come?"

"Thanks, Alex," Rachel replied with a smile, "but I think we'll stay here."

Alex ran off. Ava quickly flew out from behind Kirsty's hair.

"Let's keep looking!" she said.

The three friends continued searching the woods. Rachel was concentrating so hard on looking around, she was startled when a rabbit ran past her. With a smile, she  watched the rabbit hop into his hole near the roots of a tree.

Then Rachel's heart began to thump with excitement. There, caught on the roots of the tree, was a sparkling satin bag.

"I found it!" Rachel gasped.

Ava and Kirsty hurried over to Rachel, but before they could grab the bag, they heard footsteps. They immediately all slipped behind the tree closest to them.

But to their horror, the goblin they'd
seen a little earlier had appeared.

"Yes!" the goblin cried with glee as
he spotted the bag. "I knew I'd find it
again!"

"We have to stop him—" Rachel
began.

"Wait!" Kirsty clutched her arm.
"Someone's coming."

As the goblin went to pick up the bag,
Peter ran down the path.

"Got you!" he
said with a smile,
grabbing the
goblin by the
arm. "You're
out!"

"Let me go!"
the goblin complained as Peter led him

away. He hadn't had a chance to pick up the bag. "I'm not playing!"

But Peter didn't pay any attention. Ava and the girls shared a relieved smile as Peter and the goblin disappeared.

"Now's our chance!" Ava whispered.

They rushed out from behind the tree. But before they reached the bag, they heard even more footsteps.

"It might be Peter coming back," Ava pointed out. "Let me turn you into fairies, so you won't be spotted!"

With one swish of Ava's wand, Kirsty and Rachel were showered with fairy dust.

Immediately, they shrank down to Ava's size, using their glittering fairy wings to zoom up and hide behind a tree branch with their friend.

"Oh, no!" Rachel gasped in horror. "It's the *other* goblin!"

The second goblin began to search around the trees while Ava and the girls all held their breath. Suddenly, he spotted the bag of sunbeam dust and gave a shout of joy.

"I found it!" the goblin yelled. He grabbed the bag and jumped up and down. "Hooray! Now we won't be in trouble with Jack Frost after all!"

There was the sound of someone running, and the other goblin rushed through the trees.

"Look, I found the magic bag," the second goblin declared. He proudly dangled it in front of the other goblin's face.

"Then we've got to get out of here right away!" the first goblin panted. "I barely escaped that silly man!"

"We have to get my bag back," Ava said anxiously as the two goblins hurried off. "What should we do?"

"I think I have a plan!" Kirsty replied.

Green
Dust

"Ava, maybe we could distract the
goblins with *another* bag," Kirsty
explained. "A bag that really catches
their eye?"

Ava thought for a moment. "I can do
that!" she said with a smile.

She flicked her wand, and a cloud of
magical sparkles drifted onto the path in
front of the goblins. Instantly, a green

satin bag appeared.

"Look!" the goblin holding Ava's bag shouted. "Another bag—and it's *green*!"

The goblins picked up the bag and closely examined it.

"It has a picture of two handsome goblins stitched on the front," said the goblin holding Ava's bag. "And, look—it's *us*!"

Ava and the girls tried not to laugh.

The other goblin opened the bag, and a puff of green dust floated out.

"I like *this* bag much better," he said. "The green dust is just like the sunset."

"This must be the bag Jack Frost wanted us to look for all along!" the first goblin agreed. "Let's leave the other one here and take this one instead." He was about to drop the bag of sunbeam dust on the path when the other goblin clutched his arm.

"Wait," he said. "Maybe we should take both bags to Jack Frost."

Ava and the girls glanced at one another in horror.

"Do you think so?" the goblin with Ava's bag asked doubtfully. "I really think Jack Frost would like this green one the best."

"OK," the other goblin finally agreed.

Ava, Rachel, and Kirsty breathed sighs

of relief as the goblin finally dropped Ava's bag on the path. Then the two of them went happily on their way, taking the green bag with them.

Ava, Rachel, and Kirsty laughed as they swooped down from the tree. Ava touched her wand to the bag and it immediately shrank to fairy-size.

"Thank you so much, girls!" Ava cried. She hugged her magic bag happily. "This means that sunsets all over the fairy and human worlds can be beautiful and colorful again. Now, you'd better get back to Camp Stargaze."

With a wave of her wand, Ava made Rachel and Kirsty human size again. Then they hurried through the Whispering Woods.

As they followed the path to the

campsite, Peter appeared. Ava
immediately hid in Rachel's pocket.

"Found you!" Peter exclaimed with a
grin. "You're the last ones. Everyone else
is back at the camp."

Rachel and Kirsty shared a secret
smile as they followed Peter along the
path. When they reached the edge of the
Whispering Woods,
Ava fluttered out
of Rachel's
pocket again.
Staying out of
sight of the other
campers, she
opened her magic
bag and sprinkled
a handful of

shimmering golden dust in the air.

"Now you'll see what a real sunset
should look like!" Ava whispered, giving
them each a quick hug. "Thanks again
for your help. I know the other Night
Fairies will be coming to see you very
soon!"

And then, in a flash of sparks, Ava
vanished and returned to Fairyland.

Kirsty and Rachel gazed up at
the sky. All the campers—kids *and*
parents—clapped and cheered as the
green sunset slowly began to fade. Soft

shades of pink, orange, and gold began to appear until the whole sky was filled with beautiful color. Then the sun began to sink slowly and steadily beyond the horizon.

"It's the end of our first day at Camp Stargaze, Rachel," Kirsty said with a smile.

"But it's the start of a whole new fairy adventure!" Rachel added, her voice full of excitement. "I wonder which Night Fairy we'll meet next?"

RAINBOW magic

THE NIGHT FAIRIES

Rachel and Kirsty have helped Ava.
Now it's time to help

Lexi
the Firefly Fairy!

Join their next nighttime adventure
in this special sneak peek. . . .

A Face in the Bushes

The sun was just setting and the evening
was growing cooler at Camp Stargaze.
Rachel Walker zipped up her fleece and
tucked an arm through Kirsty Tate's
to keep warm. Rachel and Kirsty were
best friends, and their families were on
vacation together for a week. Exciting

things always seemed to happen when
the two girls got together. So far, this
vacation was already looking like
another very magical one!

Kirsty and Rachel were gathered with
about twenty other kids at the edge
of the campsite. There was going to be
a special nighttime walk, and everyone
was chatting happily as they waited
for it to begin.

"Is everyone ready? Let's go into the
Whispering Woods!" called Peter, one of
the camp counselors.

Kirsty and Rachel walked with the
rest of the group into the forest. It was
cool and dark underneath the leafy
trees. Kirsty turned on her flashlight and
pointed it ahead. The tall trees swayed
in a gentle breeze, and their leaves really

did seem to make a whispering sound.
"It's creepy being here in the dark, isn't
it?" she said to Rachel.

"Yeah, it is," Rachel replied, glancing
around. "It makes you wonder what's
hiding in those shadows."

"*Whoooo-oooo-oooo!*"

Rachel and Kirsty clutched at each
other as they heard a ghostly wailing
behind them. They spun around to see
two boys, Lucas and Matt, laughing so
hard they were doubled over. "Gotcha!"
Matt cackled.

"Your faces! You looked terrified!"
Lucas added, his eyes sparkling with
mischief.

Kirsty and Rachel laughed, too, once
their hearts had stopped racing. Those
boys! Then Kirsty had an idea, and

winked at Rachel. "Oh, my goodness!" she said, pretending to gasp in fright. "Look up there—those two glowing eyes. They're staring down at us!"

The boys gazed at the tree where Kirsty was pointing—and now it was their turn to look scared. "No way!" Matt yelped in alarm. Shining out of the darkness were two gleaming lights that looked exactly like the eyes of a wild animal. "What do you think it is? A mountain lion?"

"Hmmm," said Rachel, pretending to think. "It looks like it's a really dangerous . . . *firefly*. Actually, two!" She and Kirsty giggled. The glittering lights in the tree were only a couple of flickering fireflies—there was nothing scary or dangerous about *them*. . . .

RAINBOW magic™

There's Magic in Every Series!

The Rainbow Fairies

The Weather Fairies

The Jewel Fairies

The Pet Fairies

The Fun Day Fairies

The Petal Fairies

The Dance Fairies

The Music Fairies

The Sports Fairies

The Party Fairies

The Ocean Fairies

The Night Fairies

Read them all!

HiT entertainment

www.scholastic.com

www.rainbowmagiconline.com

RMFAIRY4

SPECIAL EDITION

Three Books in Each One— More Rainbow Magic Fun!

■SCHOLASTIC
www.scholastic.com
www.rainbowmagiconline.com

HIT entertainment

RMSPECIAL